Alexander Asenby's
Great Adventure

Stephen J. Brooks

with illustrations by Rajesh

**L**ate, late each and every night,
While his parents peacefully slept,
Alexander Asenby awoke wide-eyed,
And quietly, silently crept.

Across his cluttered room, and
Over the rickety floor,
Until he had finally arrived
At the magical closet door.

He opened the door just a crack,
A bit hesitant at first,
He peered into the blue darkness,
And shivered, fearing the worst.

Yet Alexander knew the fairies,
Would need their heroic knight.
So he mounted his fearsome dragon
And prepared for his nightly flight.

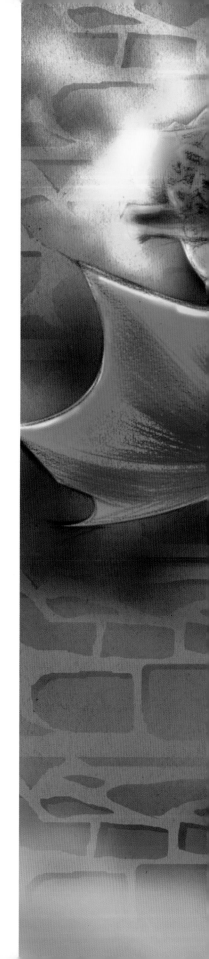

Atop his fire-breathing friend,
With sword and shield held high,
Alexander flew through the closet's wall,
Soaring off into the starry night's sky.

Into the darkness they flew,

With Alexander holding on tight.

Zooming past comets and shooting stars,

'Til they came to the end of the night.

here at night's end, a castle
Stood alone at the top of a mountain,
With a moat of flowing hot lava,
Hungrily fed by a fiery fountain.

lexander circled the castle twice,
Then landed his marvelous beast.
He was met by the cheering fairies,
Who had prepared a welcoming feast.

"Hooray for our brave, fearless knight!"
They shouted and they cheered.
But soon a silence fell over all,
As the king of the fairies appeared.

"The ogres and the trolls are back,
There's no time for fun and games!
They are out there ravaging the town,"
The king very grimly explained.

"T hen this great feast shall have to wait,"
Alexander sternly commanded.
"Quickly, bring me my dragon,
And my sword and my shield," he demanded.

So he mounted his fire-breathing dragon
And bravely rode off to fight.
To save the magical kingdom
From its terrible and dreadful plight.

s he neared the edge of town,
He saw the hideous creatures.
With their sharp teeth, big horns, warts,
And other such nasty features.

hey were stomping about and crushing,
Tearing, ripping, and biting.
Alexander, perched high on his great beast,
Loudly shouted to them, "Quit fighting!"

The ogres and trolls looked up;
All eyes mirrored their fright.
For this wasn't to be the first time
They had battled this heroic knight.

The dragon spewed his blazing fire.
Alexander raised his sword in the air.
Together they charged the monsters,
Who quickly fled in despair.

Alexander Asenby gave chase,
As the monsters ran in fear.
His dragon roared a ferocious roar,
While the townspeople let out a cheer.

Alexander and his heroic dragon,
Knew their nightly task was done.
They returned to the welcoming castle
To join in the feast and the fun.

A party was thrown in their honor
With yummy cakes and cookies to eat.
The fairies celebrated the victory,
While the monsters mourned defeat.

s the celebration came to an end,
Alexander knew the time was right,
To climb atop his dragon's wings,
And return to their home for the night.

Alexander thanked all the fairies,
The dragon let out a loud roar.
Then together they returned once again,
Back through the closet door.

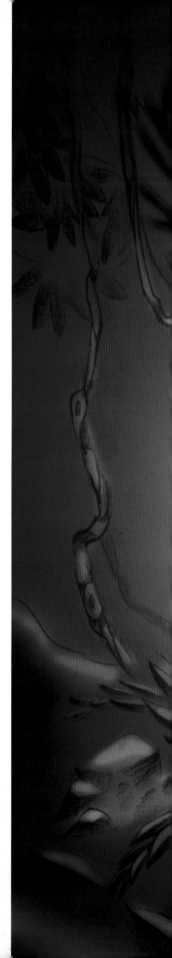

To my son Alexander,
whose tremendous growth and determination under
difficult circumstances inspires me daily. If you follow your
dreams and listen to your heart, anything is possible.

SAN: 256-5995

ISBN: 0-9769017-2-2

Library of Congress Control Number: 2005904544

Library of Congress Cataloging-in-Publication Data
Alexander Asenby's Great Adventure/written by Stephen J. Brooks
Summary: Alexander Asenby travels through a magic portal
on the back of a dragon to save the fairies.
ISBN 0-9769017-2-2
1. Fantasy - Juvenile 2. Dragons - Fiction 3. Fairies - Fiction
4. Stories in rhyme.
I. Brooks, Stephen J.
II. Title.
III. Series

PURPLE SKY PUBLISHING
PO Box 12013, Parkville, MO 64152
www.purpleskypublishing.com

Design and layout: Jonathan Gullery

Printed in China